The Tale of Taliesin

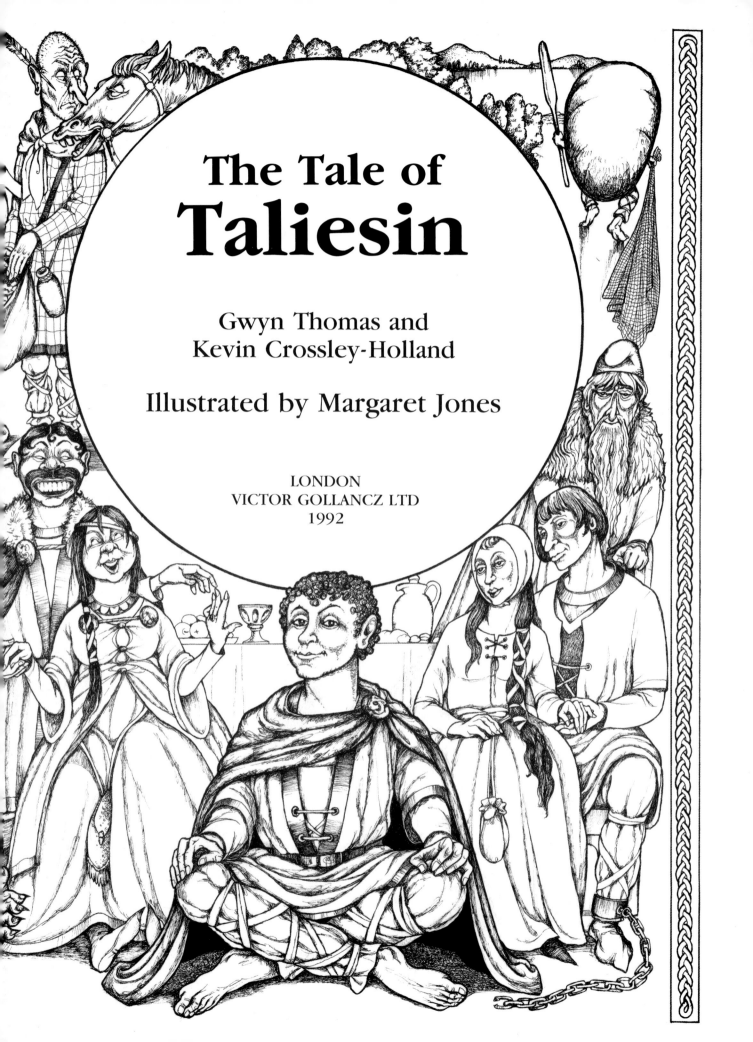

The Tale of
Taliesin

Gwyn Thomas and
Kevin Crossley-Holland

Illustrated by Margaret Jones

LONDON
VICTOR GOLLANCZ LTD
1992

THE STORY OF CERIDWEN'S CAULDRON

nce upon a time, when King Arthur was still gathering his knights about the Round Table, there was a witch called Ceridwen. Ceridwen was highly skilled in sorcery and magic. In fact, she was so skilful that everyone was afraid of her and took great care how they talked to her. She had to be handled with a knife and fork, as they say, for if someone annoyed her she would think nothing of changing him into a frog or a hare for a week or two. And, as everyone knows, being changed into a frog or a hare is not a very pleasant experience – especially if you don't like water or lettuce.

Ceridwen was married to a nobleman called Tegid the Bald. They lived in Llanuwchllyn in North Wales, and Tegid owned much land in that region. Indeed, he owned the lake called Tegid. Tegid and Ceridwen had two children, a son called Morfran and a daughter called Creirfyw. Creirfyw was the most beautiful girl in the whole wide world, but Morfran, poor soul, was the ugliest young man in the whole wide world, and his name, which means 'Sea Crow', was no help at all to him. He did have a nickname, Afagddu; but, if anything, that was even worse than his proper name for it means 'Hell'. So this son had a rather unfortunate choice of names – Morfran or Afagddu. Neither his appearance nor his name did a lot for Morfran's temper: he was the most ill-tempered and unpleasant person in the universe – and that at a time when the competition for being ill-tempered and unpleasant was particularly strong with creatures about like Ysbaddaden the Chief Giant, the Black Witch and the Twrch Trwyth. But compared to Morfran, every other ill-tempered person seemed as good-humoured as Santa Claus.

Ceridwen was very worried about Morfran – everyone is someone's child, as they say, and this one was hers. Like many a mother she thought, "What will become of this boy? He's ugly and obnoxious and thoroughly unpleasant. There's no chance of his becoming a knight and going to King Arthur's court. He would pick a quarrel with everyone there within half an hour. What can I do?"

4

You may well be wondering, "What kind of a witch is this who can change people into frogs and hares and can't make her own son beautiful?" And if you are, you have hit on Ceridwen's weak spot. Although she was a very capable witch, she was not capable enough to change the features of anyone in her family for the better. She could have changed Morfran's face for the worse; she could have turned him into a frog. But even Morfran would have found it hard to thank her for that.

Ceridwen had been worrying about her son for a long time when she had a bright idea. "Why don't I change him into an intelligent and wise man, one skilled in prophecy?" she asked herself. "A man like that would be accepted to the court of any king, however ugly and unpleasant he is!" According to some people, this was how civil servants came into being and, according to others, how teachers came into being – but the old, old book where this story is found does not say anything about this.

So Ceridwen explained her bright idea to Morfran.

"Fine," said Morfran, in his surly way. "Better than being a frog."

Then Ceridwen consulted an enormous old book she had – written in Latin so no one would understand it. She stared at this book for days on end. She ran a long nail over the lines and stopped when she came upon any charm that seemed promising. For example, when she came upon the lines, 'For lightening one's darkness', she read very carefully but had to give up because she did not understand the word 'batterius'. Another line which made her pause and read the spell was: 'How to win friends and influence people'. But she had to move on when she saw that a dinosaur tooth was required for she knew full well that dinosaur teeth were very hard to come by.

Ceridwen was beginning to despair when, one day, her long nail stopped by the words: HIC INCIPIT INCANTAMENTUM – 'Here beginneth the spell . . .' What spell? 'How to make the stupid wise.' She read on:

INGREDIENTS

The following plants at the time of the year when they grow:

3 ounces of Parsley in August
7 ounces of Wild Organy in July
14 ounces of Garlic in September
3 ounces of Dandelion in July
7 ounces of Comfrey in April
1½ ounces of Wormwood in June
3 ounces of Yellow Rattle in May
1 ounce of Ivy in December
A dash of Mint in August. . .

And so on – this story would be much too long if all the ingredients were listed here.

HEAT: Boiling.

METHOD

1. *You will need a great iron cauldron. Fill it with water, boil the water, and keep it on the boil constantly on a big log fire.*
2. *Soak the plants, as appropriate, for one night before placing them in the boiling water at the appointed times of the year.*
3. *Stir the brew with a large wooden spoon every six hours.*
4. *Carry on doing this for a year and a day.*
5. *At the end of this time, place the Stupid One on the right hand side of the cauldron so that the essence of the brew, that is to say three drops, will fall on one of his fingers.*
6. *He should put his finger in his mouth. After swallowing the three drops, the Stupid One will be wiser and more learned than anyone in the whole world.*

P.S. It is forbidden to drink any drop of the brew remaining in the cauldron as it is PURE POISON.

P.P.S. Good luck!

"Here we are! This is the solution to my worries," said Ceridwen. "Morfran! Morfran! . . . MOR-FRAN!" She had to shout three times because, on principle, Morfran would not do anything willingly no matter who asked him.

"What, mam?" he asked.

"Go to Gofannon, the great smith, and ask him to make me a big iron cauldron. About twelve feet round."

"Why, mam?"

"Because this is the way to de-stupefy you and to de-idiotize you."

Morfran looked amazed. He scratched his head.

"What's that you said, mam?" he asked.

"This is the way to make you intelligent and pleasant – so you can go to King Arthur's court."

"Do I have to fetch this cauldron? Why can't Creirfyw do it?"

"You're the Stupid One, aren't you? You're the Unpleasant One? So you can fetch the cauldron. Off with you, *now!*"

Away went Morfran to Gofannon. And three weeks later, three oxen dragged a cart to Tegid and Ceridwen's house and in the cart was an enormous cauldron.

"How much do I owe you?" asked Ceridwen.

"Fifty pounds," said Gofannon.

"How much!" asked Ceridwen.

Silence. Gofannon swallowed hard.

"How much did you say . . . my little hare?" asked Ceridwen again.

"Hare!" said Gofannon and a picture of himself hopping about with two long ears came into his head. "Well . . . since I know you: thirty pounds."

"Thirty pounds!" said Ceridwen, as if she were about to faint. "How much did you say . . . my little frog?"

"Frog!" said Gofannon, and again a picture of himself, yellow and goggle-eyed and up to his neck in a cold pool hopped into his head. "Hum . . . well . . . twenty pounds?" he said hesitantly.

"Very reasonable," said Ceridwen. "Tegid, pay!"

Now Ceridwen needed someone to look after the cauldron – Ceridwen's Cauldron as it was now called. She decided to employ a blind man called Morda to start the fire under the cauldron and tend it for a year and a day, and throw the plants into it, and to stir the brew. Ceridwen chose a blind man because she feared anyone who could see would be much too interested in what was going on and discover some of her witch's secrets. But after she had chosen a blind man she realized that she would have to get someone to help him, to fetch wood for him and to guide him around the cauldron. Since Ceridwen was very arrogant, she thought there would be little risk if she could find a 'yokel' – that's the word she used – to help Morda.

"Some ordinary person – a real vegetable – would be ideal," she said to herself. "Someone like that, brought up with cows and dung, would not be any the wiser even if he did see what plants I put in the cauldron. I'm told that there's an extraordinarily ordinary person in Llanfair Caereinion. I'll get him."

The extraordinarily ordinary person from Llanfair Caereinion was Little Gwion.

"Couldn't be more suitable," said Ceridwen. "Just look at him! He's as stupid as an ox. The very man for the work."

Then a square stone wall was built to enclose the fire, and the wall had gaps in it so the wind could blow through it and fan the flames. A strong iron grid was placed on top of the square wall and then, on top of that, the great cauldron. It was filled with water. By the side of the square a small platform was built for Morda to stand on, and throw the plants into the cauldron, and stir the boiling brew with a large wooden ladle. Little Gwion was kept busy carrying loads of wood until there was a large pile within reach of the cauldron. Before the fire was lit, Ceridwen walked round the cauldron three times, chanting in Latin:

> "Hubble bubble
> Cauldron bubble,
> Hubble bubble,
> Cauldron bubble,
> On this brew I'll cast my spell.
>
> Hubble bubble
> Cauldron bubble,
> Hubble bubble
> Cauldron bubble,
> In its brew will wisdom dwell.

Hubble bubble
Cauldron bubble,
Hubble bubble
Cauldron bubble,
By this brew all will be well.
Morfran, by my mighty spell,
Will be the wisest man of all:
By this brew all will be well."

After this, Little Gwion placed a layer of dried heather under the cauldron and piled firewood on top of it; then Morda lighted the fire. Then everyone went to it, hammer and tongs – Gwion kept the fire roaring red with sections of tree trunks and sturdy branches, and he guided blind Morda; Morda himself put the plants in the cauldron and stirred the brew every six hours; Ceridwen flew hither and thither on her swift broom to fetch plants at the appropriate times. Steam arose from the cauldron and various smells were carried here and there over north Wales, as the wind blew. The people of north Wales sniffed the breeze and said, "There's wormwood in the cauldron today, no doubt. How long is that Gorgon going to inflict these terrible stinks on us?" But though they complained amongst themselves about the cauldron, of course no one dared say as much as a word to Ceridwen herself.

After busying themselves in this way for a year, Gwion, Morda and Ceridwen were extremely tired. Of the three, Ceridwen was the most tired, she felt exhausted. Since the essence of the brew – the three magic drops – was all but ready, she called to Morfran:

"Morfran, Morfran . . . MOR-FRAN! Come here, will you!"

"I don't want to," said he, in case he should please anyone by doing so.

"See here, Morfran," said Ceridwen. "If you don't come here, you'll lose your chance forever of being more wise and knowing than anyone else."

"Oh! What's this?" Little Gwion said to himself. "Is this why I've worked and sweated for a whole year? To make this numbskull less of a fool?"

"Morfran, stand here!" Ceridwen made a mark on the ground on the right-hand side of the cauldron with her heel, "Stand on that and don't you dare move."

"Well, if I must," said Morfran grudgingly.

"You must, love," said Ceridwen, "and if you move an inch from there I'll skin you alive!"

"Yes mam," said Morfran, for he knew that his mother was not one to be disobeyed.

"That's fine, dear," said Ceridwen. "Morda – stir that brew! Gwion, fetch some wood for this fire – and hurry up."

And they did exactly as Ceridwen told them.

"Ah, well!" said Ceridwen. "That's that! It'll be the dawn of the big day in half an hour. I'll take a short rest now, since I've nothing better to do – I'll be busy enough before long."

Ceridwen lay down within sight of the cauldron. "Oh how pleasant!" she said to herself. "How very pleasant . . . and I'll be able to see . . . what's happening . . . from here . . . Pleasant . . . most pleasant . . . very pleasant . . . indeed . . . in . . . deed . . . in . . . deed . . ." Before she had fully completed her sentence, Ceridwen was fast asleep. And after a while, she began to snore.

"Gwion . . . Gwion," said Morda.

"What is it?" asked Little Gwion.

"Has one of the pigs got out of the sty?"

"Pigs escaped? No. Why?"

"I hear grunting."

Ghghghghgh, phooooo; ghghghghgh, phoooooo: Gwion listened and that's the sound he could hear too.

"That's not a pig, it's the mistress," he said. "The old sow's asleep and snoring."

"I do believe this brew's becoming thicker," said Morda. "It's quite difficult to stir."

"Perhaps it's time for the drops to come out of it," suggested Gwion. "The sun is rising and this is the day when things are supposed to happen."

13

"I hope so," said Morfran, who had been listening to them. "I'm tired of standing here like a statue."

"All right, then," said Gwion. "Don't stand there!"

As he said this, Gwion gave Morfran a hard shove; and since Morfran was not expecting anything of the kind, Gwion caught him off balance. He sailed through the air like a clay pigeon and landed on his head in the wood-pile.

At that very instant the cauldron gave the most terrible screech anyone had ever heard, and the three magic drops jumped out of it and fell on the forefinger of Little Gwion's right hand.

Water from a kettle that's been boiling for three minutes is hot enough: this brew had been on the boil for a year and a day and so it was hotter than hot. It was very hot indeed! If you burn your finger the natural thing to do is to put it in your mouth. This is exactly what Little Gwion did, and in doing so, he swallowed the three magic drops. In that instant he came to know all things, all things that have been, that are, and are to be.

Of all the knowledge in Little Gwion's head it struck him that one matter was more important than all else: namely, that this place was not too safe for him. Ceridwen would very soon wake up and then, woe betide him! So, as the wisest man in the world, Little Gwion decided to beat it. And off he went.

When the cauldron gave the terrible screech, it split in two. The contents poured out, and because they were pure poison, a river nearby was polluted. Later that day, the horses of a nobleman came to that river to drink, as was their custom. As they drank they began to fall down dead, one after the other. And because of this that river was called Afon Gwenwyn Meirch, the River of Horse Poison.

The cauldron's screech woke Ceridwen. She was rather confused at first, like anyone who has just woken. Then, as she saw Morfran's feet thrashing about in the wood-pile, she began to sense what had happened. She got up and went over to Morda, took hold of his large wooden ladle, and hit him on the head with it so that he saw many beautiful stars. After he had come to his senses, Morda said, "Who did that?"

"Ceridwen did," said Ceridwen.

"Why?" asked Morda.

"Because all my efforts over the past year have been wasted," she said.

"That's not my fault," said Morda.

Morfran's voice came from the wood-pile, "It was Little Gwion's fault."

"That little nobody!" shouted Ceridwen. Then she added, "I ought to have known better – what else would you expect of an ordinary nobody? Which way did he go – the twit?"

"That way," said Morfran, kicking with his feet towards Llanfair Caereinion.

"I'll show that scum what happens to those who cross me," hissed Ceridwen. Then she jumped on her broom and away she went after Little Gwion.

Little Gwion's legs were so short it wasn't long before Ceridwen caught sight of him.

"Help," said Little Gwion as he saw her hurtling towards him. "The old bag's here already. I wish I were a hare."

No sooner had the word 'hare' come into his head than Little Gwion felt his ears growing longer, his legs becoming the long hind quarters of a hare and his hands becoming paws. The three magic drops had given him the powers of a wizard!

"Thank heaven," he said, and began to leap up the side of the hill. "Ceridwen's broom will never go fast enough to catch a hare."

But Gwion's joy was short-lived. Ceridwen belonged to the highest order of witches and catching a hare was no problem at all for her.

"Just wait, little hare," she said.

> "Abracadabra
> Abracado
> I'm in a hurry and I want to switch,
> I'll change myself into a greyhound bitch."

At once Ceridwen turned into a black greyhound bitch. Her thin nose was like the point of an arrow and she whistled along as if shot from a bow.

Gwion found himself – in the form of a hare – running downhill towards a river. As you know, a hare goes more slowly downhill than uphill –

because his hind legs are stronger than his front legs. By the time Gwion had reached the bank of the river, the greyhound bitch's sharp teeth were snapping at his tail.

"Into the river!" Gwion said to himself. "I'll be a fish." He jumped from the river bank in the form of a hare, turned into a fish in the air, and fell with a splash in the water.

"Abracadabra
Abracadee
Now it's time for another switch,
I want to be an otter bitch,"

said Ceridwen. And she, too, gave a great leap from the river bank, turned into an otter bitch in the air, and fell with a splash into the water.

Gwion sped on, wiggling his fish tail like a fan. But fast as he swam, and he swam very fast, he was conscious of a brown form gliding nearer and nearer to him. He tried stopping, turning quickly, swimming upstream, turning quickly again and then moving downstream with the water; but the teeth of the otter bitch were still only a few inches from his tail.

"Away!" Gwion said to himself. "Bird: I'll be a bird." He broke from the water in the form of a fish jumping for a fly, for a moment he hung, a bright flash in the air, and then he turned into a bird and soared into the sky.

"Abracadabra,
Abracadaw
Now it's time to fly and squawk;
To catch that bird I'll be a hawk,"

said Ceridwen, leaping from the water, hanging in the air, wet and furry and then turning into a hawk. She pulled herself upwards, upwards with her strong wings.

Whip, whap; up, down; right, left; Gwion — in the shape of a bird — attempted to avoid the hawk, and the witch drew ever nearer, nearer to him. He could feel her wings disturbing the air behind him as he tried to escape. Then he felt one of Ceridwen's sharp talons touching his tail-feathers.

"O, mam, what shall I do!" Little Gwion said to himself. "I'm done for!" Then, out of the corner of his eye, he saw a heap of cornseed far down below in a farm yard. Gwion clapped shut his wings and fell like a stone. But Ceridwen did the same. Gwion saw the earth leaping up towards him. At the very last instant he opened his wings and landed in the heap of cornseed. As he touched down he said, "A seed, a seed, I'll be a seed." And at once the bird turned into one little seed in the midst of the heap.

Ceridwen did not close her wings in time. She crashed like a sack of potatoes into the heap so that seed was scattered everywhere.

"Well done!" thought Gwion, making himself small amongst the thousands of seeds about him. But then he heard Ceridwen saying her magic words:

"Abracadabra
Abracaday,
Feather me and then, oh! then,
I'll be a black, red-crested hen."

The next thing Little Gwion – the seed – saw was a fat, black, red-crested hen eyeing him ferociously and clucking in a most unpleasant manner.

"Guawk, guawk," said Ceridwen – the hen – and she scratched a heap of seeds with a threatening yellow talon. "Guawk, guawk, guawk."

Gwion tried to make himself even smaller than a seed. But the hen scratched the cornseed again and Gwion saw her angry, unblinking eye. "Guawk," said the hen. And the next thing Gwion knew was that he was moving down a dark slide and landing in a heap of other seeds and two earthworms. He found himself in a most unpleasant place – inside a hen!

Then Ceridwen immediately changed herself back into her own shape. "You won't get out of there in a hurry!" she said.

But it was from there that the seed came – nine months later – in the form of the most beautiful baby you ever saw.

For nine months, Ceridwen had been thinking what unspeakable things she could do to this Little Gwion when he was born. For some weeks, she particularly liked the idea of roasting him; then she thought of frying him slowly; then . . . But when the baby was born, she couldn't do any of these things to him, because he was so beautiful.

"Oh dear me!" said Ceridwen. "I can't kill him . . ." She looked at the baby and began to croon, "And what is mummy's little snugglumps doing? . . . Oh, my beauty!"

Who should put his head round the door just then but Morfran!

"Who are you calling snugglumps?" he asked. Then he looked at the baby and answered his own question. "It's that fat pig, isn't it. Have you forgotten who it is? Don't you remember what this nasty lump of blubber did to me?"

"Ah! yes indeed," said Ceridwen. "If it weren't for him, you would be in King Arthur's court now, revered by all. You would be the wisest, the man with the most knowledge in the whole world instead of being the ugliest monster in creation."

"Yes," said Morfran. "So let's have less of this snugglumps. Let's roast him or fry him until his horrible belly bursts out and his guts curl up."

"I'll tell you what I'll do," said Ceridwen. "I'll make a skin bag, a leather bag, and grease it well and then we'll put this baby in it and throw it in the river."

"Why don't you roast him?" asked Morfran.

"Well . . . Well . . ." Ceridwen looked at the baby again. "And what are you doing now, my little snugglumps . . ."

"There you go again!" said Morfran, and he was extremely annoyed. "Snugglumps, snugglumps! Have you forgotten that I'm your son – and not this pink lump?"

"Right. You're right," said Ceridwen. "We'll chuck him in the water in a skin bag."

"Yes . . . yes . . . if you're not going to roast him or fry him or stew him, that will have to do," said Morfran.

When the skin bag was ready, the baby was put in it.

"Morfran," said Ceridwen, "here he is. Throw him into the lake." She was thinking of Llyn Tegid, or Bala Lake. Then the baby might have been carried down the River Dee and into the sea near Chester – and perhaps someone would have found him on his journey and taken him out of the water.

After his mother had left him, Morfran said to himself, "He's on his way into the water, that's for sure, and a much greater water than this lake; I'll take him to the sea." And that is what happened; Morfran carried the skin bag to Barmouth and threw it into the sea there. "And that's the end of baby bumpkin!" said Morfran. "He'll be food for fish before tomorrow. Good riddance, I say!" Then Morfran went home and – if it's possible – he was even more obnoxious and more unpleasant than before.

The skin bag swayed gently, gently on the small waves near the shore. Then, with the ebb-tide, it was carried out into the great waters, where there were bigger waves and where the bag surged and fell, up and down, up and down with them.

This took place on 29th April, but no one knows the year.

THE FINDING OF TALIESIN

ot far from the place now called Tre Taliesin in mid Wales there was, many centuries ago, a weir. A weir is a half-circle of stones or of wooden branches on the sea shore, with its outer curve facing the sea and its open arms reaching towards the land. The incoming tide covers the weir, and then, when the sea ebbs, a pool remains within the half-circle of the weir for a while. Then the water in this pool gradually drains out through the wall of the weir, leaving the sea's gifts inside it. Thus a weir is a very good contraption for catching fish!

23

A nobleman called Gwyddno Garanhir (Longshank) owned a weir on the beach between Dyfi and Aberystwyth – the Weir of Gwyddno. On May Day every year there was a hundred pounds' worth of fish in this weir. Now one year Gwyddno promised his son, Elffin, that he could have all the fish in the weir on May Morning. The reason for this was that Elffin had been rather foolish, and thrown a great deal of money around while keeping company with some young men at the court of King Maelgwn of Gwynedd. He was heavily in debt. He hoped to pay all the people from whom he had borrowed with the hundred pounds he would get for the fish. So early on May Day he was waiting, impatiently, for the tide to turn so that his father's servants could fetch the fish for him from his father's weir.

At last the tide turned and the walls of the weir began to appear.

"It won't be long now, sir," one of the servants said to Elffin.

"I hope it won't. I'm stiff with cold," said Elffin.

"Here we are, sir, the pool's beginning to drain out through the walls. This is where we find one hundred pounds' worth of fish every May Day," said the servant.

"I can see the water draining from the weir," said Elffin, "but I don't see any sign of a fish."

"You just wait now sir," said the servant. "They're all gathering in one great shoal in the water that's left behind."

But as the water slowly drained away, there was no salmon, no whiting, no cod, no plaice, no herring, no crab, no periwinkle, nothing.

"And where are the fish 'in one great shoal'?" asked Elffin, very annoyed. "Where are they? Where?"

"We-ell sir . . . I'm not . . . I'm not . . ."

The servant tried to fish about in his head for some words but, at that moment, his brain was as empty as the weir.

"Well what, you fool?" asked Elffin, as prickly as a hedgehog. "Where are the fish?"

The servant went fishing in his brain again and hooked the word 'Unfortunate'. He began to repeat the word over and over: "Unfortunate . . . Unfortunate . . . Very unfortunate, sir."

"Unfortunate indeed, you idiot," said Elffin, as if the unfortunate servant were to blame for the lack of fish in the weir. "Why aren't there any fish here? Why? Why?" And he began to see the 'friends' from whom he had borrowed so much money gathering about him like hungry sharks, all teeth.

The servant stood there opening and shutting his mouth – looking a bit like a fish himself – but without finding any other words. Then he saw something black caught in the bottom of the weir wall and he found his voice, "Look, look sir, over there – something black . . . Maybe it's a new kind of fish."

"A new kind of fish indeed! It's a lump of nothing, more than likely!" said Elffin. But for all that he gave the black thing another, closer look.

By now, the servant had reached it and picked it up.

"It's skin, sir," he said. "Well greased."

"I can see that," said Elffin, still very annoyed. "I'm not blind."

"See what's inside it, sir."

"That's what I intend to do," said Elffin, bringing out a knife and beginning to cut through the skin bag.

"Careful, sir," said the servant. "In case there's something valuable inside it."

Elffin paused. "Will you shut up, you fool," he said. "I know what I'm doing."

Elffin went on cutting the skin very carefully. Then he began to open the skin, just as carefully. The first thing he saw was a forehead (*tâl* in Welsh), a most beautiful (*iesin*) forehead.

"Well," he said in amazement, "there's a fine forehead (*tâl iesin*)!"

And a young voice answered, "Then let me be called Taliesin."

Before the words were all out, the servant had covered fifty yards. Then he stopped and shouted to Elffin, "Let it be, sir. Leather bags are not supposed to talk! Let it be!"

"It's not the leather talking, you idiot," said Elffin. "It's this baby inside the skin. He's saying his name will be Taliesin."

"A baby talking!" shouted the servant. "Let it be, sir, that's as bad as a leather bag talking. He's a magic baby, leave him alone!"

"Fool!" said Elffin to himself. He took the little baby out of the skin bag and carried him over to his horse. He put him gently in the basket behind him on the horse – one of the baskets he had hoped to fill with valuable fish. And since there was not a single fish in any of the baskets, Elffin was still very cross and had rather a 'What can I do?' look about him. Baby Taliesin was so small that Elffin had his horse go slowly and gently. And then the baby began to speak again; and this time in verse.

> "Fair Elffin, stop your weeping,
> And don't blame me for being
> Here in Gwyddno's Weir today:
> I came in my own magic way.
>
> Fair Elffin, stop your moaning,
> And don't continue groaning;
> You have no cause to be so sad
> Now I have come to make you glad.

Fair Elffin, when you know my power
You will bless the magic hour
You took me from the empty weir
To be your good companion here."

Elffin was truly amazed and he began to be less cross and more cheerful. And all the way home Taliesin babbled poetry to him.

After he had arrived home Elffin went straight to his father Gwyddno.

"Well Elffin, how did it go?" said Gwyddno.

"No fish, dad," replied Elffin.

"No fish! On May Day!" Gwyddno was amazed.

"But, dad, I found something better than fish," said Elffin. "This!"

"And what is this?" asked Gwyddno.

"A poet."

"Oh, poor lad!" said Gwyddno. "Of what worth (*tâl*) is a thing like that to you or anyone else?"

The baby didn't like this. It butted in and said, "Of great worth (*tâl iesin*). I'm worth more than anything ever found in your weir."

Gwyddno was astounded. He could not speak for a while. Then he said,

"You can talk and you're so little!"

"I can," said Taliesin. "I can say more than you can ask me."

"I told you, didn't I?" Elffin said to Gwyddno.

"This one's like every other poet I know," said Gwyddno. "A big mouth!
Ask any poet about anything at all and he'll tell you, 'I can do it, I can do it!'
I know these poets, full of words and good for nothing."

"But I'm different," said Taliesin.

"All right, then," said Gwyddno. "Tell me where you came from."

"That's easy," said the baby,

"Before I was Taliesin
I was in the sea in
A bag being carried away
For one night and one day.
I was born before then
To a witch called Ceridwen,
And before then was a corn seed
Swallowed as part of the feed
Of a black, red-crested hen,
And for a time before then
I was a bird in the sky
When I had no choice but to fly
From a hawk which pursued me.
Before then I had to flee
As a fish from an otter
Slipping swiftly through water.
Before then I was a hare which
Was pursued by a bitch,
And before all that commotion
For a while I was Gwion
Who had a peculiar itch
To fool Ceridwen the Witch.
And before I was Gwion
I was three drops in a cauldron.
And there you have, in rhyme,
My passage through time."

"Indeed, you have something very special here," Gwyddno said to Elffin.
"This is no ordinary poet; this one seems to know everything."

"Correct," said Taliesin.

"I know all things, you see:
What was, what is, and what will be."

28

"It may well be that this is of more worth than a weir full of fish," said Gwyddno. "Take care of him."

"I'm going to give him to my wife to bring up," said Elffin. "Ellyw will be delighted."

And that is what happened, Taliesin was lovingly brought up by Ellyw and Elffin. He was a wonder boy, and from the minute he came to Elffin's house, Elffin's luck changed; he was able to pay all his debts and became quite a rich man.

ELFFIN'S TROUBLES

When Taliesin was thirteen years of age, Elffin was invited by his uncle, King Maelgwn of Gwynedd, to pass Christmas at his court in Degannwy. Such an invitation was a great privilege for Elffin: it was only great and important people who were invited. So off he went to King Maelgwn's court.

There were all kinds of lords and ladies and all sorts of important people from various parts of Wales at King Maelgwn's court. And one night they were all in the great hall of the court enjoying a splendid feast. There was an abundance of food and drink there and everyone felt very happy.

In order to please Maelgwn, some of the important people began to flatter and do what they could to please him. It was Cecil Hoggit, a long thin stretch of a man with thin yellow hair and a reddish moustache who started it all. As it happened, he was sitting next to Elffin.

"Oh! how pleasant it is to be here. Charming! Enchanting! Splendid!" said Cecil Hoggit. "King Maelgwn is the richest king in all the world. So splendid! So mighty! Just one of his rings is more valuable than the castle of any other king!"

"True, true, oh how true, my dear friend!" said Sunny Dylan, a short thickset man who was also sitting not far from Elffin. "But if Maelgwn is the richest of all kings of the world, he's the bravest too, the most valiant, the best warrior of all the warriors of the world. Oh! how lucky we are to be defended by such a strong and glorious king!"

At this, a young lady with cross-eyes called Guennever cut into the conversation, "Certainly, certainly; nothing more certain. But if King Maelgwn is rich and valiant he is also the most handsome, the most beautiful, the best-looking King in the whole world. Ooh! He's an angel! Isn't he an angel?" she said turning to Elffin. Elffin said nothing.

"You never said a truer word, madam," said Cyledr the Smooth, a tall, dark knight. "And you yourself – if I may say so – are a most beautiful angel. But though your words are true, I must question whether Maelgwn is the fairest one in all the world."

"What!" said one.

"Consider your words, sir!" said another.

"Are you mad, sir?" asked a third.

"No, indeed not," said Cyledr, "Maelgwn is not the fairest in all the world."

"Shame on you," said Ysbaddaden, son of Brian, a very small, small man. "If I were three years younger, sir, I'd give you the worst hiding you've ever had. I never heard such an insult!"

"Half a minute, friends," said Cyledr. "Maelgwn is not the fairest in the world . . . but his wife, Sannan. Our most noble queen is the most beautiful, the most gentle, the most pure person in the whole world."

"Ah! well sir," said Ysbaddaden, "I can agree with that – almost. I would say Maelgwn, our king, and our gracious queen, Sannan, are as handsome and beautiful as each other, and certainly are more beautiful than anyone else in the whole world."

Then a large chorus of voices joined together to praise King Maelgwn:

"What man is as brave as Maelgwn, and what soldiers are braver than his soldiers?"

"Who has finer and swifter horses than Maelgwn?"

"Who has poets that are half as wise and learned as those of our king?"

"What other poet can hold a candle to his chief poet, Heinin? There's no one like him!"

Elffin had been sitting quietly at the table, growing more and more angry as he heard all this nonsense. But now he could hold back no longer, and he said:

"I know full well that no one but a king should compare himself with another king. I'm no king but, if I were, I would say my wife is as pure as Sannan, our queen. I would also say that I know of a poet – my poet, Taliesin – who is more wise and learned than any of the king's poets. And I would also say that my horse is swifter than any of the king's horses."

The hall became as quiet as a grave. There was not a sound – not even the sound of Maelgwn's poets swilling their beer.

"What did Elffin say just now?" asked King Maelgwn. "I didn't hear him clearly."

First there was a silence for a few seconds. Then a whole crowd got up, and shoved and jostled their way towards the king's table, each of them eager to be first.

"Oh most high king," one began. "I heard him plainly . . ."

"And so did I – I was directly in front of him . . ." another cut in.

"I heard him best of all, your majesty," interrupted another. "My right ear – which is my good ear – was barely ten inches from his mouth . . ."

"Silence! Quiet!" said the king's chamberlain. Everyone became quiet. "One at a time!" said the chamberlain, and he turned to Ysbaddaden, son of Brian. "You first!"

"Oh sir, I can barely utter the shameful words this Elffin spoke," Ysbaddaden began, "but, begging your pardon, O most exalted lord, Elffin said that his wife – and everyone knows she's a brazen hussy, sir – he said his wife is as pure as our most dear queen."

Before Ysbaddaden had paused for breath, Cecil had begun to speak, "And that's not all, most sublime one! He said that his own poet – Taliesin – some nobody no one had heard of, is wiser and more learned than your poets! The very idea, your majesty!"

"And I heard him say," said Guennever, "that his own horse is swifter than your magnificent horses, O king!"

"He did," said someone else.

"I heard him too," said another.

"And I."

"Me too."

"Silence!" shouted the chamberlain, for things were getting out of hand again. Everyone became quiet. There was not a wheeze to be heard as Maelgwn began to speak, "So that's how it is, Elffin? Is that it? Equal to – no better than – your king? Did you say these things?" There was a great silence, and then Elffin said,

"Yes, O king."

"Why did you say them?"

"Well . . . well . . . because they're true."

"True! True!" said Maelgwn, his voice quiet and menacing. "Well, you can cool your heels in jail. You can stay in prison until we prove how 'true' your words are!"

Elffin had no chance to say anything else. Four hefty soldiers marched him down to the castle dungeon and wound fetters and chains about his feet and hands. Elffin could only drag himself around with great difficulty. Then the iron door of Elffin's cell was slammed shut with a bang that resounded down the cold and dark tunnels of the dungeon. And then there was great silence.

TALIESIN HELPS ELLYW

King Maelgwn had a son called Rhun, and this Rhun was a hot lecher and lover of women. The king's counsellors decided to send him to test how pure Ellyw, Elffin's wife, was.

"Your task is to bring back some proof to the king, your father, that this Ellyw is not so pure and innocent as Elffin claims," said the chief counsellor, Morgan, to Rhun.

"That'll be no trouble at all for me," said Rhun with a sly grin.

"Very likely," said Morgan, "but you'll have to bring us some proof of your success, remember that."

"I'll think of something," said Rhun giving Morgan a little wink. "You stick to counselling and I'll stick to loving – each to his own thing!"

Rhun set off on his horse, with a number of servants from Maelgwn's court in Degannwy. He whistled happily at the thought of the delightful task that lay ahead of him.

As Rhun was setting off, Taliesin came to Ellyw. "Mistress," he said, "some evil is about to happen."

"Evil? What evil?" asked Ellyw.

"Our master's in prison in Maelgwn's castle," said Taliesin.

"Good heavens!" said Ellyw. "In prison! Whatever for?"

"For talking too plainly to the king," said Taliesin.

"Are you sure?" asked Ellyw.

"Mistress!" said Taliesin. "You know me. You know I'm always right and know what *is* to happen as well as what *has* happened."

"I do," said Ellyw.

"Master's said that you are as pure as Queen Sannan," said Taliesin. "He's also said I'm wiser and more learned than Maelgwn's poets and his horse is swifter than Maelgwn's horses."

"What on earth came over him to say such a thing?" said Ellyw. "Everyone in the king's court either keeps his mouth shut or opens it to praise the king."

"Master can be excused for telling the truth," said Taliesin. "But listen now: Rhun, the king's son, is on his way here to try to bring shame on you."

"That dirty pig!" said Ellyw.

"If he's a dirty pig, he's a dirty pig that women like," said Taliesin.

"Well! I don't like him, that's for sure," said Ellyw. "The low down trickster! He'll get nowhere by coming here."

"Fine, mistress," said Taliesin, "But remember that he appears most affable and, besides that, he has some magic powder that he uses to help him and make things easier."

"Powder?"

"Yes, powder to put in the drink of whichever girl he's after. The powder makes people sleep."

"Yes, no doubt!" said Ellyw. "Well! Neither he nor his powder will come into this house."

"You have to welcome him," said Taliesin. "You don't know what they could do to Elffin if you shamed the king's son by refusing to welcome him."

"Oh! What shall I do?" said Ellyw.

"This is what you'll do, mistress," said Taliesin. "Have one of the kitchen maids – Diridano, perhaps, she's always happy with the men – have her wear your clothes and put some of your rings on her fingers."

"What for?"

"As Rhun has never seen you, he'll suppose that Diridano is you, and then, if anything happens, well ..."

"Good idea," said Ellyw, "we'll get the smith to make one or two of my rings larger to fit Diridano's fingers."

"That large ring, Elffin's ring – the one with his name on it – will do as it is," said Taliesin.

"Yes," said Ellyw. "It's too big for me. That's why I wear it on this chain."

On the day when Rhun and his servants arrived, a Saturday, Diridano was elegantly dressed in her mistress's clothes and her mistress's rings shone brightly on her fingers. Ellyw was dressed as a maid. The moment Rhun saw Diridano (or 'Ellyw' as he thought) he said to himself, "There'll be no trouble here, I'm sure of that; but I don't know how it would be if I had to try my luck with this maid – she's a real sourpuss if ever I saw one."

Rhun and his servants were given a warm welcome and after they had washed, they were entertained at a great feast that night. Everyone enjoyed the feast – though the maid 'Diridano' was clumsy and spilt sauce on the sleeve of Rhun's best shirt. He was rather annoyed about this at first, but then he began to play around and crack jokes. "A shirt, a shirt, my kingdom for a shirt!" he said. And then, "This maid is rather saucy!"

At last everyone except Rhun and 'Ellyw' went to bed to sleep. This was when Rhun began to make advances to 'Ellyw' and to whisper endearments in her ear. Sweet words, such as:

"My love is like a red, red rose."

"Come live with me and be my love."

"Ere you were born was Beauty's summer dead."

"The brightness of your cheek would shame the stars."

"Let us live and love, 'Ellyw', and care not a fig for all the talk of wizened, strait-laced old men."

'Ellyw' laughed joyfully when she heard Rhun, and said, "Yes, yes! More, more!"

After a while Rhun began to think he had no need for the magic powder that night but, in order to be perfectly sure, he put some in 'Ellyw's' drink without her noticing. After the two of them had spent a pleasant hour together she began to sleep as soundly as a dormouse.

"Now!" Rhun said to himself. "Proof! What proof? Ah! This ring with Elffin's name on it."

Then Rhun tried to take the ring off 'Ellyw's' little finger until he was blue in the face. "It's too tight," he said to himself again and again. "Too tight! What shall I do?"

Then it struck Rhun that 'Ellyw' was so fast asleep she could feel no pain. At once, as quickly as he could, he cut off her little finger and put it, and the ring on it, in his purse. Then Rhun woke his servants and they stole away in the darkness, step by step, by the light of the moon.

After he had reached Maelgwn's court in Degannwy, Rhun told his story to his father and to his father's counsellors. "Well done!" said Maelgwn. "It couldn't be better. And now we'll send for Elffin. He too can hear the story and swallow his words!"

Elffin came up to the hall, dragging his fettered feet.

"Ah! Here you are Elffin," said Maelgwn. "We've called you to hear a little story about your wife, a story about her and Rhun . . ."

"There's no story about my wife and that one," said Elffin.

"Oh! yes, there is," said Maelgwn. "A very romantic little story. I'm going to ask Rhun himself to tell it to you."

"Yes, well, this is how it was," said Rhun, and he went on to tell the story. He told it as colourfully as he could, and concluded by raising a piece of cloth on the table. Beneath it was 'Ellyw's' little finger with the ring on it.

"Come nearer, Elffin," said Rhun, "so you can see the proof. Here's your wife's finger with your very own ring on it – positive proof that your dear wife doesn't love you half as much as you thought."

Elffin came to the table and his chains clanked and rattled. He examined the finger carefully.

"We all sympathize with you," said Maelgwn. "But it's very foolish for anyone to believe his wife and think she's faithful and loving. That's not how women are; it's not their nature. This finger is proof enough of that."

"This ring," said Elffin, "I can't deny it's mine . . ."

"There we are – confess that we're right!" said Maelgwn.

"But," said Elffin, "but this finger, it's not my wife's finger."

"How's that?" asked Rhun. "I assure you, it's the finger of the mistress of the house."

"But not the mistress of my house," said Elffin.

"You're only saying that to console yourself," said Rhun "and to try and deceive us."

"No," said Elffin, "and I'll tell you why. This finger was never part of my Ellyw's hand. For one thing, this ring; this ring was too slack to fit even on

39

Ellyw's thumb. But as you can see, it can't even be pulled off the little finger of the woman who had this finger."

"A lie, a lie!" said Rhun.

"All right, then! Why didn't you take the ring off the woman's finger and bring it here? That would have done well enough as proof," said Elffin.

"It wouldn't come off," said Rhun. "But the ring on the finger is more proof than the ring by itself."

"More proof that you've been with the wrong woman, yes," said Elffin.

"The woman who had this finger was the mistress of the house," said Rhun scowling.

"She was pretending to be the woman of the house," said Elffin. "However, there's a second proof that this is not Ellyw's finger. Every Saturday night she has a habit of cutting her nails before going to bed. Now, look at this little finger! See how long the nail is – this woman hasn't cut her nails for a month."

All of Maelgwn's counsellors gathered round the table and looked closely at the finger. "True enough," they said, and, "Indeed, this nail hasn't been cut for quite a while."

"Perhaps she forgot to cut her nails," said Maelgwn.

"She cut them the Saturday before I came here," said Elffin. "Not one of her nails could have grown as long as this one."

"A lie! A lie!" said Rhun who was, by now, beginning to realize he had been deceived.

"Thirdly," said Elffin, "if you look closely at this finger you'll see traces of dough in the joint."

Once again Maelgwn's counsellors looked hard at the finger. "This is true," they said, and "Yes, there is a little dough in the joint."

"Ellyw has never kneaded dough since she's been my wife," said Elffin. "Gentlemen, you wouldn't expect a lady, the mistress of the house, to go to the kitchen to knead dough!"

"Perhaps she happened to get hold of a lump of dough," ventured Rhun, but he wasn't even able to convince himself, let alone anyone else.

"If these reasons don't prove that my wife is faithful," said Elffin, "well then, send for her and you'll see she has all her fingers!"

"Less of this nonsense!" shouted Maelgwn. By now he realized Rhun had been duped and made to look a fool. He was livid with anger but, as often happens, he did not turn his wrath on the cause of his wrath. Instead, he chose to punish Elffin. "Take this prisoner back to his cell and keep him there in darkness. Away with him!"

"But why?" asked Elffin, since he had proved himself to be right.

Maelgwn had no good explanation for the punishment, so he tried to hide that by shouting, "Don't you speak like that to me, you insolent dog! You've got more to prove yet! You boasted that your poet is better than my poets, your horse swifter than my horses. Away! Take this prisoner away from here, NOW!" And Elffin was taken away with his chains clanking.

TALIESIN AND MAELGWN'S POETS

Although he had not been near King Maelgwn's court Taliesin knew what had happened there. He told Ellyw all about it, and finished by saying. "So master's still in a dark prison. But don't you despair, mistress! He'll be set free in due course. I'll go to Maelgwn's court to help him."

"But how on earth can you do that?" asked Ellyw. Taliesin replied:

> "I shall go on my way
> To Degannwy to stay
> In the hall of the king,
> At his court shall I sing.

His poets — to his surprise —
I'll defeat, for I'm wise.
No one can compete
With me, and no feat
At all is beyond me:
All this will you see.
I'll win Elffin his freedom
From King Maelgwn's dungeon."

"I know how clever you are but this is a most difficult task," said Ellyw. "Maelgwn has twenty-four poets, and his chief poet Heinin is very learned indeed. You're just a boy — are you sure you'll succeed?"

"Of course I shall," said Taliesin. "There's no doubt about it. Don't worry. And now farewell!" And off he went to Maelgwn's court.

Taliesin arrived at the court just as a great feast was about to begin and many important people were going into the hall to take their places at the tables according to their eminence. Taliesin stole in unnoticed and went to a quiet corner by the door through which the poets would enter to sing to the king.

After the feast Maelgwn's chamberlain got up, struck his staff on the floor and shouted, "Silence! Everyone!" Everyone became quiet. The chamberlain proceeded, "It is now time for one of the most important ceremonies of the day, it is time for our most eminent and most glorious King Maelgwn, dragon of the Isle of Britain, brightest sun in the firmament of kings, most generous of all men, to be praised by the poets. Let the poets be summoned to the presence of our most high and glorious king."

The door was opened, and a voice called out, "Let the poets come to the presence of the most high king Maelgwn." At this the twenty-four poets entered, one after the other, each attempting to appear as wise and learned as he could. Taliesin crouched in his corner, but as they went by he extended his lower lip and, playing on it with his fingers, he made a noise: "broom broom broom broom". Not one of the important poets took the least notice of him. Each of them took his place before the king and bowed low.

"Let it be known," announced the chamberlain, "to everyone here in the presence of His Highness, King Maelgwn, that the king consents that the poets may sing his praise. Let the first poet approach, our chief poet Heinin, to sing his praise to Maelgwn."

Heinin came forward slowly and with dignity. He stood before the king, he coughed to clear his throat, he nodded to the harpist to indicate that he should begin to play his harp. Then Heinin opened his mouth, pushed out his lower lip, put his fingers to his mouth and began to play "broom broom".

Some of the lords looked at each other, puzzled as to how to respond to this noise. Was it a new way of singing? Should they praise Heinin for his originality? Or what? They were still puzzling when Maelgwn interrupted the performance with a shout that was loud enough to raise the roof. "RUBBISH!"

After this the lords at the tables also began to shout: "Rubbish!" "Shame!" "I've never heard such trash!"

"Is this fool drunk?" asked Maelgwn in a loud voice. "Have the poets been at the beer again?"

Heinin abandoned his performance. And the instant he did so he was able to talk normally. "Your majesty," he said, "we are not drunk."

"Out!" shouted Maelgwn.

"But your majesty, we haven't sung you our praise poems," said Heinin.

"Out, out!" shouted the lords.

But poets are not the sort to depart without singing their poems, as everyone knows. "Your majesty!" said Heinin. "My lords! You all know that we, the poets, have worked immensely hard, immensely hard, to compose the most wonderful praise poems to the high king of all Britain. I beg you, don't ask us to depart without giving yourselves the opportunity to enjoy these splendid songs."

"One more chance then," said Maelgwn grudgingly.

"I thank your majesty," said Heinin. "You and these noble lords and ladies here will not be disappointed. Listen carefully now and enjoy some of the century's most important poems."

Everyone became quiet. Heinin drew himself to his full height. A figure of great dignity. He coughed to clear his throat. He nodded to the harpist. The hall was filled with beautiful harp music. Heinin opened his mouth, he pushed out his lower lip and began to play "broom broom" on it with his fingers.

"Shame!" "An insult!" "Out with the fool!" shouted several important persons and they began to thump the tables and stamp their feet.

"Silence! Silence!" shouted the king's chamberlain. And everyone at once fell silent. Maelgwn's face turned red, and scarlet, and purple, and at last he roared, "FOOL! IDIOT! UNCIRCUMCISED TWERP!" ("What's that?" murmured many of the important persons to each other.) Maelgwn went on to shout "OUT!" in various keys, each one grinding in the ears of every lord, lady, poet and servant in the hall.

Any sane man would have sprinted for the door but, you see, these were poets and, in addition, poets who had not had an opportunity to sing their poems. They stood their ground like a row of heifers, glaring at the king, and he continued to bellow "OUT!" until the place echoed.

When the king saw this gang were still unmoved, he passed a metal dish to one of his servants. "Give that idiot a thump on the head," he said. The servant took the dish, went up to Heinin, and gave him such a crack that he saw stars and fell on his back like a pancake.

"The rest of them will run for it now," thought Maelgwn. But no. Heinin sat up, and got on to his knees: "O most magnificent king, and lords of the realm," he said, "we are not drunk, we are not to blame for this, there's some . . . some spirit here which defeats us. And if I'm not mistaken, these evil effects are coming from that corner." Heinin pointed to the corner where Taliesin was sitting, and everyone turned to look at the thirteen-year-old boy.

"Bring that boy here," said Maelgwn. Two of his servants went to fetch him, and Taliesin stood before the king.

"Who are you, boy?" Maelgwn asked Taliesin. And Taliesin replied:

> "I am, o great king,
> Chief poet to Elffin."

"So you're Elffin's poet! Where do you come from?" asked Maelgwn. And Taliesin replied:

> "I have been in my prime
> Since the beginning of time."

"Since the beginning of time!" remarked Maelgwn. "What's the meaning of such words?"

Taliesin went on to say this:

> "Before being drops in a cauldron
> That were swallowed by Gwion
> I have been in this world
> A long time – I'm very old.
> 'I have been' and 'I am'
> Since the making of Adam.
> I marched with a banner
> In the army of Alexander.
> I saw the destruction
> Of Gomorrah and Sodom.
> I have been in Asia
> In the Ark with old Noah.

I have been many a generation
Here before the birth of Gwydion.
Three times my abode
Has been the prison of Arianrhod.
I have been called many things
In my many beginnings,
I was lately called Gwion
But from now on I'll be Taliesin."

"Your majesty," shouted Heinin, "this is a mad fool! He wants us to believe he's as old as the world – that he's been with old heroes like Alexander; been with old, old men of the Bible like Noah; been with our ancient Welsh, Gwydion and Arianrhod! He's mad, your majesty, a real idiot!"

"Wait, Heinin!" ordered Maelgwn. Then he turned again to Taliesin and asked, "What is your business here?" And Taliesin replied:

"Elffin, who is Gwyddno's son,
Is held here in your prison.
I am Taliesin, the best
Poet of all in the West,
I'm here to save Elffin
From his suffering, O king."

"Chief poet of the West!" shouted Heinin. "This one's clearly out of his mind, your majesty! Everyone knows that I'm the chief poet of the West – and the East too, if it comes to that." Heinin rounded on Taliesin: "What right have you to call yourself a poet, let alone steal my title and call yourself the chief poet of the West? Chief poet of the West indeed! Can you compose in twenty-four metres? Can you count syllables? Have you served your apprenticeship as a poet? Can you tell me who was the father, the grandfather, the great-grandfather, the great-great-grandfather of our most illustrious king Maelgwn?"

"I can do what I will," said Taliesin. "And if you're so clever tell me what this is:

"What is it that's so old –
Older than the Flood that drowned the world –
And has no veins and no blood,
And no feet and no head,
Yet runs through the trees
As lightly as the breeze,

Crosses a sea without boat,
Crosses river, crosses moat?
It flies through the sky
And with no wing can climb high.
Its condition is good
Though it touches no food,
This being is so strange
Its age does not change.
Ponder, wise poets, and tell me then
What was here before the creation of men?"

"Has no veins and no blood!" said Heinin. "This is not a person."

"Perhaps it's a snake," suggested one poet. "It can move through the trees though is has no feet."

"And it can, of course, fly though it has no wings!" said Taliesin sarcastically.

"Oh! . . . Yes," said the poet.

"The answer is simple," said Heinin. "There is no such thing; it's a duffer's question."

"And that's a duffer's answer," said Taliesin.

"Duffer! Witness, witness your majesty, that this . . . beardless boy called me a duffer! Don't you know that I am the leader of the poets of the Island of Britain and all neighbouring islands? And do you know why? Do you know I've won more bardic chairs than any other poet?"

"Wooden chairs?" asked Taliesin.

"Of course!" replied Heinin. "Solid wood."

"Just like your head," said Taliesin.

"Witness, witness what this scurvy little knave called me," shouted Heinin.

"Answer my question," said Taliesin.

"How can I, or anyone else, answer a question to which there's no answer?" asked Heinin.

"Here's the answer," said Taliesin. "It has always existed, it has no legs or feet and yet it moves where it will – what is that but the WIND."

"No feet . . . moves . . . has always been . . . Indeed, Heinin, he's right," said one of the other poets.

"A fluke," said Heinin. "That was just a fluke."

"No fluke," said Taliesin. "The truth is that you, the poets, are not what you should be; you are ignorant where you ought to be wise, and have no knowledge where you ought to be learned. All you think about is guzzling food and swilling ale.

"These poets, they misuse their art,
Pretend and flatter, play a part,
Don't know the truth, there's no denying,
So used, by now, to fawning and lying.
By night, boozing; by day, sleeping;
They laze about – except when eating!
Birds fly, fish swim, and that is good,
All living things work for their food
Except for rogues and thieves and poets."

"Shame! Insult!" shouted Heinin, livid with anger. "Your majesty! Throw this insolent cur into the dirtiest and darkest dungeon in your kingdom. Let him rot there!"

"Less lip!" said Taliesin. "Don't you know I can call forth spirits from the deep and call forth storms and whirlwinds?"

"Call them, yes, but will they come when you have called them, eh!" mocked Heinin, and all the poets began to laugh and say, "Quite right, Heinin," and "You tell him what's what. The little upstart!"

Taliesin endured this for a while, and then he chanted this spell:

"Now wake the wind, now wake the wind,
Wake the wind and fury find;
Now wake the wind and furious come,
Shake this castle, come, now come."

As Taliesin said these words, the poets and everyone else in the hall fell silent. And when he had finished there was no sound to be heard. Then they all heard the sinister whistle – low and quiet at first – of the wind in the sea down below. They heard the sound of wooden buckets being blown about the court of the castle, and doors and wooden shutters slamming. Then a whirlwind hit the court, it shook the foundations, it picked up objects and hurled them about. The ceaseless wind made a sound like wave upon wave being thrown up against the stone walls of the castle. All the poets scrambled under the tables and began to fight and squabble for the best places.

Through the growling and whistling of the wind, Maelgwn shouted, "Calm this storm, Taliesin! Calm the storm!"

"When Elffin is here and free," replied Taliesin.

"Servants, go and get Elffin!" shouted Maelgwn, and his words were snatched away by the storm. Then four soldiers stooped into the whirlwind and fought their way down to the dungeon. And as soon as they opened the door of Elffin's cell the wind dropped as suddenly as it had risen.

One by one, the poets came out from under the tables. Heinin was the last to come. He tried to flatten his hair which stood up on his head like the quills of a porcupine and, mustering what dignity he could, he said, "Your majesty, it's time for us to go now. When there is no feast, that's the time of day when we study. We have a great longing to study." Then, looking at Taliesin, half-fearful and half-scornful, he added, "This is the only way we can still be as wise and as learned as we have always been."

Then, like a band of lame camels, the poets went out through their special door.

Elffin arrived in the hall, still in chains. Taliesin went to his master and held him. He sang a song:

> "I now behold my master Elffin
> Still chained, still fettered, still demeaned;
> I proclaim that he will be
> Unchained, unfettered and set free."

Thereupon the chains about Elffin's feet broke. And after Elffin had stretched, and flexed his muscles, and recovered the use of his legs, he and Taliesin walked up to Maelgwn.

"Your majesty," said Elffin, "you see that two of the things I said – about my wife and about my poet – are true. What about my best horse? Shall we find out whether he is faster than your best horses?"

In truth, Maelgwn was none too keen for his horses to race against Elffin's horse after what had happened, but he had to keep face in court.

"Agreed," he said. "Next Friday at mid day we'll meet for the race, at Morfa Rhianedd (Maiden Bay). I shall be there with my twenty-four horses."

"All right," said Elffin, "and I'll be there with my best horse."

THE HORSE RACE

he following Friday a large crowd gathered on Morfa Rhianedd, all of them eager to see how things went in the race. Maelgwn's twenty-four horses were well known and acknowledged to be the fastest horses in the kingdom. No wonder, for they were splendid animals! They were large horses, some of them black, some chestnut, all shining in the sunlight, their heads bright as they pranced about, eager to run. King Maelgwn looked on them with pride from a wooden platform that had been raised specially for him and some of his noblemen.

Elffin's horse was there too. He was a grey, lively but rather small, with ears like pears and eyes like yellow flames. His name was Llwytyn (Grey). His rider, a young red-haired lad, stood by his side holding his bridle, and talking with Elffin. Taliesin was not there.

The race track had been marked out on the shore, and it was a long one. The aim was not to race from the starting point to the other end of the shore, but to keep going — to gallop back from the far end to the starting point, then back again to the far end and so on.

A number of men were walking around and looking at the horses. Then, every so often, they would go up to a little man with a thin face like a ferret who stood to one side. There were large squares on his clothes and he

53

wore a red scarf about his neck. The men pointed to one or another of Maelgwn's horses, and handed him pieces of gold or silver. Not one pointed towards Elffin's horse. Not, that is, until Taliesin arrived. Then some of the important people, who were in Maelgwn's court when it was hit by the high wind, came to have a look at Llwytyn, and some even put some money on him.

Taliesin went up to Llwytyn's rider, a lad called Iorwerth, son of Beli and known as Iori (Yoree). Taliesin had hazel twigs in his hands, twenty-four of them, and all of them burnt black.

"Now then," Taliesin said to Iori, "put these under your belt."

"Under my belt?" said Iori. "Things such as these under my belt will hardly help me ride a horse. To tell you the truth, they'll be a great hindrance."

"Take them," said Taliesin quite sharply, "and do as I tell you."

"Do I have to, master?" asked the lad turning to Elffin. He was not at all eager to follow Taliesin's instructions. "He's younger than I am," he said.

"You do exactly as he tells you, Iori," said Elffin.

Iori pushed the twigs under his belt.

"Let Maelgwn's horses start before you do," said Taliesin.

"Start before me!" Iori nearly choked. "I came here to try and win this race. Master, he knows no more about horses and racing than the man in the moon."

"Even if he tells you to ride back to front," said Elffin, and he said it very firmly, "you're to do exactly as he says."

"Wait here while I put a penny or two on one of Maelgwn's horses!" said Iori spitefully.

Taliesin took no notice of Iori's objections. "As you catch up with Maelgwn's horses," he said, "you're to take one of these twigs from your belt and whip the crupper of the horse next to you, and then let the twig fall. Do you understand?"

"I understand the words," said Iori. "It's just that I don't believe them. Anyone who knows a thing about horses would know I won't catch up with Maelgwn's horses like that – not unless this clever boy means to supply my horse with wings."

"You do as he says," Elffin said again, slowly, patiently, and very, very definitely.

"As you catch up with one of Maelgwn's horses, whip him on the crupper with a twig and then let it fall," said Taliesin. "And when you've done that to all the other horses, keep going until Llwytyn stops. Drop your cap on that spot and leave it there."

"And then I'll dig and find a treasure," said Iori. "Just like that!" By now, he was quite convinced that Elffin and Taliesin were both entirely mad.

"Yes!" said Taliesin laughing. "That's exactly what will happen."

Iori raised his eyes to heaven. Then he mounted Llwytyn and said, "Well, at least I've managed to get up on his back without sticking a twig up my . . ."

"That'll do, Iori," said Elffin. "You do as Taliesin told you."

"Come on then, Llwytyn," said Iori. "After winning this race, for our second trick we'll jump over the moon; and as we go by, we'll give her a slap on the bum too – with a twig!" Iori turned Llwytyn's head towards the starting point where Maelgwn's horses were already walking about, ready to begin.

The horses all moved into one line. Then Maelgwn stood up. "Remember, keep to the rules – go up to the far end and back, then back again, just as you've been told. Start when I drop this handkerchief. Ready! One, two . . . " Maelgwn dropped the handkerchief.

The king's twenty-four horses leaped forward at the same time, and galloped along the strand, kicking up pieces of turf in a sandy shower over Iori and Llwytyn – they were still at the starting point. Many of Maelgwn's men began to laugh, and those who had backed Llwytyn said farewell to their money.

At last Llwytyn started forward. "He's understood the purpose of this race at last," shouted one man, and those were the last words Iori heard as he bent low on the neck of his horse.

To the far end, back to the beginning, to the far end, back again – so it went on for some time. Then Llwytyn caught up with one of Maelgwn's horses. Iori was so surprised he almost forgot to slap the horse on its crupper with a twig. After whipping the horse he let the twig fall. That horse soon stopped quite exhausted. Then Iori caught up with another horse, whipped it, and let the twig drop, then another and another until there was only one of Maelgwn's horses left. This was a shining black horse, many hands high. By now, a white froth of sweat hung from his mouth, but he still kept going, kept going. But, metre by metre, Llwytyn caught up with him. Then Iori struck him on the crupper with the last twig and let it fall, and the shining black horse slowed to a canter, a trot, a walk, and pulled up, exhausted. But Llwytyn kept going for another two hundred metres. Then he too slowed down and stopped. Iori dropped his cap on the spot, dismounted and gave Llwytyn a kiss on his sweating forehead.

Though King Maelgwn tried to smile, he was furious and, after 'congratulating' Elffin, he and his men went straight home. That night in the court, many men felt the lash of his tongue and the hard toe of his boot.

Elffin and some of his servants came with Taliesin to the spot where Iori had dropped his cap. The servants carried spades. By now Iori had changed his tune and was very eager to please Taliesin. "Here, sir, here exactly is where I dropped my cap. It was here, sir, that Llwytyn stopped. The best little horse that ever was!"

"We should dig here," said Taliesin. And the servants began to dig, biting into the sandy soil.

"Good going, lads! Keep at it!" said Iori, enthusiastically.

After a while, there was a clink. The spade of one of the servants had struck against something hard.

"This is it, lads. It's here!" said Iori.

"You'll see a cauldron in a moment," said Taliesin. "Lift it carefully."

"Careful with this cauldron now, lads," said Iori. "Well done, well done!"

Slowly and carefully, the servants lifted the cauldron from the hole and set it on solid ground. There was a large lid on the cauldron and an enormous lock on the lid. "Iori," said Taliesin, "what about opening this lock?"

"A pleasure, sir," said Iori, getting hold of a crowbar. He put the tip into the clasp of the lock, and pushed. For some time nothing happened. Then, very slowly, the lock began to give until, quite suddenly, it snapped open. Everyone gathered about the cauldron.

"Open it," Taliesin said to Elffin.

Then Elffin took hold of the lid and slowly lifted it. Gems and gold and silver! Everyone stood in silence, gazing at the cauldron full of the most amazing treasure.

Elffin cupped his hands and lowered them into the cauldron and filled them with gems and jewels; then he let it all flow back through his fingers into the cauldron. He turned to look at Taliesin. He could not say anything.

"There's a fine payment *(tâl iesin)* for picking me out of that weir and bringing me up," Taliesin said to Elffin. "A cauldron full of treasure!"

"A fine payment indeed!" Elffin said. Then Iori gave a great cry, "Hurrah!" and all the servants began to laugh and shout and dance happily around the cauldron.

The hole that was dug to find the cauldron has filled up with water and become a pool. It was called Pwllbair (Cauldron Pool).

THE END OF THE TALE

After King Maelgwn had overcome his disappointment at losing the horse race, and acknowledged that there were people in this world as good as himself, and things as good as his things, and recognized that Taliesin was indeed the Chief Poet of the World, he and Elffin became very good friends, better friends than they had been before they quarrelled. Elffin and Ellyw and Taliesin often visited Maelgwn's court in Degannwy. There, from time to time, Taliesin would prophesy and tell Maelgwn about things that would happen in the future. One of his most famous prophecies was about the nation of the Britons, that is to say, the Welsh:

> "They will praise their Lord in time to come,
> They will keep their tongue in time to come,
> They will lose their land for some time to come,
> But Wales will always be wild.
>
> Then Britons will, in time to come,
> Win back their lands in time to come,
> And win back their crown in time to come,
> And Wales will once more be theirs."

Some of Taliesin's prophecies were very difficult to understand, but the meaning of these words is quite clear – if the Welsh worship God then they will keep their language and their country.

After some time Elffin died, Ellyw died, and King Maelgwn died; Taliesin went from this world. But some say all he did was change his shape, as he has done since the time of Adam and Eve. Some say that he, Taliesin, is still here and with us.

First published in Great Britain 1992
by Victor Gollancz Ltd,
14 Henrietta Street, London WC2E 8QJ

A catalogue record for this book is available from the British Library

ISBN 0 575 05326 7

The illustrations and the new version of the text were commissioned by the Welsh Arts Council

Typeset by Afal, Cardiff

Printed and bound in Belgium by Proost

PRINTED IN BELGIUM BY

proost

INTERNATIONAL BOOK PRODUCTION